THE NARROWEST BAR MITZVAH

THE NARROWEST BAR MITZVAH

by Steven Schnur

illustrated by
Victor Lazzaro

•

Union of American Hebrew Congregations
New York

To AHM

whose ark has sheltered many a damp soul

In Loving Memory of

VINCENT CESARE LAZZARO

1959-1986

But oh! shipmates! on the starboard hand of every woe,
there is a sure delight; and higher the top of that delight,
than the bottom of the woe is deep.

Moby Dick

It all began when a water main burst in front of the temple. By the time we arrived that Friday afternoon for our final rehearsal, the police had closed the street. "Probably a fallen tree," Dad remarked as we approached the flashing lights.

"They better have it cleared away by tomorrow morning," Mom said. She was almost as nervous as I was. Both of us had spent months preparing for my Bar Mitzvah. While I had been busy studying Hebrew, practicing my Torah and haftarah portions, she had been meeting with caterers, florists, and musicians, planning the menu, designing the flower arrangements, and choosing the music for the party that she and Dad were throwing after the service.

A policeman motioned us to turn off onto a side street. Dad stuck his head out of the window and asked what was wrong.

"Water main break," he replied. "You can pick up Milton Street three blocks down."

Mom leaned across to Dad's window. "We're just going to the temple. Can't we drive that far?"

"Sorry Ma'am," he answered. "At the moment there are several thousand gallons of water blocking your way. And, from what the captain tells me, a good part of that has ended up in the temple basement. You can reach the rabbi at home."

"He's supposed to meet us here," Mom said, her voice rising as it does when she gets upset. "We're expecting a hundred people tomorrow for my son's Bar Mitzvah."

"I'm afraid the building will be closed until they pump all the water out. Right now the power's shut off."

"Harold," Mom said, falling back into her seat. "Do you understand what is happening?"

"I think we've got a small problem on our hands."

I sat in the back beside my older sister Nora, too nervous to care about broken water mains and flooded basements. All that day—before, during, and after school—I had recited the blessings over and over to myself, terrified that I might mix them up when I finally stood before the congregation.

The key was to remember which started with *Baruch* and which with *Barechu*. If I got that right, the rest was simple. I knew it all by heart. But, occasionally, when feeling too confident, I began without thinking, confused the two blessings, lost my place in the Torah, stumbled

over the translation, and had to stop and begin again. "Concentrate," Rabbi Stevens reminded me last Tuesday. "You won't get a second chance on Saturday."

Dad pulled the car over, told Mom not to worry, and got out saying, "I think we'd better take a look for ourselves."

When we reached the enormous hole blocking the entrance to the temple, I knew the problem wasn't going to be solved overnight. Two fire department pump trucks were busy draining the water while workmen from the power company, bureau of highways, and water department looked on. No one knew the extent of the damage. And the water didn't end there. It had spread from the road across the grass to the temple, turning the front lawn into a great lake.

"If it got into the sanctuary, the carpet will be ruined," Mom said, looking more nervous than ever.

Over the roar of the pump trucks, Dad asked one of the firemen when the road might be repaired.

"You're looking at a week's worth of work, if you ask me," the fireman replied. "There are a dozen damaged pipes and cables down there that will have to be replaced before the hole is filled in and paved over."

Maybe missing my Bar Mitzvah wouldn't be so terrible, I thought as Dad went in search of a second opinion. I had been looking forward to being the center of attention but dreaded making mistakes in front of my family and friends. If Nora hadn't read her portion so perfectly two years ago, I wouldn't have worried as much. But I knew everyone was going to compare me to her.

As Dad returned with the same bad news from the police captain, Rabbi Stevens arrived carrying high rubber boots in one hand and a

Chumash in the other.

"This is one way to make your *sidrah* come to life," he said, surveying the damage. My Torah portion was the story of Noah.

"What are we going to do?" Mom asked in desperation.

"It's worse than I thought," Rabbi Stevens answered, slipping on his fireman's boots. "I need to retrieve a few papers from my study. Why don't you wait for me at your house. Don't worry," he said, placing his hand on my shoulder, "we're not going to let a little water prevent you from becoming Bar Mitzvah."

No sooner had we returned home than the real trouble began. When the phone rang, Dad remarked, "It's probably the rabbi." But it wasn't. It was someone speaking so loud that I could hear him across the room, crying, "It's not my fault. It was an act of God. I don't have insurance for this kind of thing. It will ruin me."

"What's the problem, Mr. Tuckman?" Dad asked, recognizing

the caterer's voice.

"Sixty chicken breasts, thirty pounds of roast beef, one hundred and twenty stuffed tomatoes—all my food, all YOUR food—ruined, spoiled. Everything is sitting in the temple kitchen. The power has been turned off, no refrigeration, water everywhere. I can't even drive in to rescue my chopped liver. It's a tragedy."

"Harold, what's the matter, who is it?" Mom asked, watching Dad's face grow dark.

"Mr. Tuckman," he said, covering the receiver. "The food."

"What about the food?" Mom's voice cracked.

"Mr. Tuckman, I'll call you back," Dad said, hanging up the phone as Mom slumped down on the couch.

"Don't tell me," she said. "It's all at the temple."

Dad nodded, loosening his tie. Then the phone rang again. Nora answered, expecting the rabbi. But it was the florist. All the flowers had been delivered to the temple that morning, before the water main break. The baskets for the tables and the large bouquet for the *bimah* were sitting under four feet of water in a basement storage room.

6

"What else could possibly go wrong?" Mom wondered aloud, rising again and pacing the room.

"You had to ask," Dad said as the phone rang for a third time. "If it's not the rabbi, hang up," Mom insisted.

"It's your mother." Dad handed her the phone.

"I could use a shoulder to cry on," Mom said. But she didn't cry, she didn't even speak. She just listened for almost a minute before finally saying, "How long did the doctor say he would have to stay in bed?"

"Is Grandpa alright?" Nora asked. Mom waved her hand to quiet her, trying to listen to Grandma. "Don't worry about that," she said into the receiver, "Alex will understand. He'll give him a private reading tomorrow night. Just make sure he stays in bed." She hung up without mentioning the flood, the food, or the flowers.

"I knew it would happen sooner or later. He's so stubborn." She looked out the window in the direction of Grandpa's house. "He tripped on those awful stairs, sprained his ankle, and almost broke his

hip. He couldn't have picked a worse time. The doctor ordered him to bed for a week. Momma says he's heartbroken about missing the Bar Mitzvah. How many times have I warned him? He's too old to be living in that crazy house. Three flights of stairs just to go from the bedroom to the kitchen. A man his age shouldn't have to go mountain climbing every time he wants a glass of water. He needs a small apartment in a warm climate. If only Momma would convince him. But after fifty years she's still as proud of his handiwork as he is."

Grandpa loved every inch of his house. He had built it himself during the Depression, calling it his ark because it had protected his family during the great storm of poverty that drowned so many people during those years. From the side it actually looked like an ark. I've never seen another house like it.

To begin with, it was only six feet wide. "I didn't have much money back then," Grandpa explained every time someone new visited. All he had was a long, narrow plot of land in the center of town and a great pile of odds and ends left there by the junkyard owner who sold him the property.

He and Grandma had come over from Poland a few years earlier,

carrying everything
they owned in a large,
black trunk. He
worked on his cousin's
farm then, tending
animals, plowing fields,

dreaming of the day he would own his own farm. But he never earned
enough money for that. Still he managed to save a few dollars, enough to
buy the land that everyone else considered worthless.

Because he couldn't build his house wide, he built it high. Some said
it looked like three railroad cars stacked one on top of the other with a
tiny caboose on top. The house was so long that Grandpa once talked of
building a bowling alley in the parlor. But it was so narrow that Dad could
stand in the middle of any room, stretch out his arms, and touch the op-
posite walls. The stairs were also narrow and very steep; only one person
could use them at a time. How, I once asked, did Grandpa get all the
bedroom furniture up to the third floor. "I made most of it myself
upstairs," he told me. "Except, of course, for the mattress. We brought
that in through the window."

Their first anniversary in the house, Grandpa bought a secondhand upright piano for five dollars. "I promised Grandma back in Poland that she would have a piano one day." He had planned ahead for it, building a great sliding barn door into one of the walls of the second-floor parlor. "All that first year Grandma kept asking me why I had built such a thing into the wall. I told her that if ever God sent another flood we'd be ready to welcome all the animals right into the parlor. You should have seen the expression on her face the day she found the piano standing there. I told her that I had carried it up the stairs on my back."

The first time Nora and I slept at Grandpa's, he pulled a rope ladder down from the third-floor ceiling, climbed up a few rungs, threw open a trap door, and disappeared. When we followed him into the tiny room at the top of the house, he said, "Welcome to the crow's nest." From there we could look out in every direction over the town. "I used to sit here after dinner, reading and watching the sunset," he told us. "I still would if Grandma didn't make such a fuss about my climbing that ladder. I've seen a lot of interesting things from here. One night I spotted a few local boys stealing pumpkins from my cousin's field. They never did figure out how we caught them." He pointed out the dry goods store that hired him after his cousin sold the farm. Beyond it stood the synagogue

which he had helped to found thirty years ago. "All that used to be farmland," he said of the new homes surrounding the temple. "One by one all the farmers disappeared."

Grandpa's and Grandma's room on the third floor faced the back of the house. The one Mom and Aunt Lilly shared when they were girls faced the front. The bathroom between the two rooms was so small that you had to stand in the bathtub to use the sink, which was fine as long as the tub was empty.

Grandpa thought his greatest achievement was the second-floor parlor. It ran the whole length of the house, almost forty feet long. In the middle, against one wall, stood an ancient cast-iron stove which had been the only source of heat until after the war. At the far end, flanked by potted palms, he had built a platform for his favorite piece of furniture, a deep Victorian-style sofa bought at a farm auction. "This was all very fashionable when your grandmother and I were newlyweds," he once told me. He knew styles had changed, but he still loved the atmosphere he had created as a young man. Most evenings he would sit back in a corner of the couch, smoking his pipe and listening to Grandma playing the piano.

After the war Grandpa became manager of the dry goods store, saved enough money to buy the empty lot next door, and told Mom and Aunt Lilly that he would build a house there for the first one who married. "Neither of them took me up on my offer," he said. "I think they were afraid I would build them a house like mine. Anyway, the

better business got, the less time I had to do the things I really loved. Maybe some day I'll build a house for you or Nora."

When Grandpa turned seventy, Mom announced that the time had come for him and Grandma to move in with us. "That's no house for people your age," she argued. "One of these days you are going to slip on those narrow stairs and break a hip."

"You'd be sick and tired of us in two weeks," Grandpa protested.

"Then at least let me find you an apartment. Something without steps."

"Climbing those stairs is what keeps us young," Grandpa smiled. He loved to tease Mom.

Still, she persisted. "Try to convince your grandparents to move in with us," Mom would say whenever I rode across town to see them. I never tried. I loved that house and I loved the way Grandpa got around. Even in his late seventies he had a way of holding onto the banister and sliding down on his heels. "Not bad for someone pushing

eighty," he would say with a grin.

When I began learning my Bar Mitzvah portion, Grandpa and I practiced together Saturday afternoons, climbing up into the crow's nest when Grandma wasn't looking. He grew up speaking Yiddish and had learned Hebrew in a *cheder*, like the other boys in his town. But he never celebrated his Bar Mitzvah. Just before his thirteenth birthday, a pogrom swept through his village, forcing his family to flee. By the time life returned to normal, five years had passed and he was too busy trying to earn a living. But tutoring Nora and me, he said, was like having his own Bar Mitzvah. He got to know our passages as well as we did.

After practicing with me for an hour, he'd tell stories about his childhood in the little Polish *shtetl* of Kolbuszowa. There his father sold tobacco, and his uncle struggled to make a living as a musician. "Uncle Aaron was a *klezmer*, he lived and breathed music. A scholar he wasn't—he could hardly write his own name—but he knew every song ever written. And, when occasionally he didn't know one, you had only to hum it and he would play it back on his clarinet before you had finished. You should have heard him play at our wedding. He could make his clarinet weep with joy."

Uncle Aaron died during the war. His memory still brought tears to Grandpa's eyes. "For your Bar Mitzvah he would have walked all the way from Kolbuszowa," Grandpa said. "That's the kind of man he was. He lived to give people pleasure. For that the Nazis murdered him. I pray you never know such times. But enough, life is too short to dwell on misery. Come."

Then he would take me around the house, each week revealing a new secret, like the two discarded railroad tracks that supported the first floor, the pulley system used to send meals up to the parlor and the bedroom, or the hidden laundry chute that ran from the bedroom to the basement. He once sent a pair of socks down and never saw them again. "I loved those socks. They were argyle. Very fashionable then. I wonder what happened to them." He often hinted at other secrets that even Grandma and Mom didn't know about, but those, he said, would have to wait.

Nora had given Grandpa the first *aliyah* at her Bat Mitzvah, and I planned to do the same. But, now that the temple was flooded and Grandpa ordered to bed, it didn't look as though he would be able to join me on the *bimah*. I felt like Noah when the rains came. Who ever thought the world could be so changed by water! But, before I had a chance to dwell on my disappointment, the doorbell rang. It was Rabbi Stevens, still wearing high rubber boots and carrying his *Chumash*.

"Rabbi, why is this happening to us?" Mom asked. "Everything is ruined." Then she told him about the food and the flowers and Grandpa's fall. "Is this God's way of punishing us?"

Rabbi Stevens smiled as he pulled off his boots. "I don't know about you, but it may be God's way of reminding me that books should never be stored in a basement. I kept meaning to move them. There must be five hundred volumes underwater."

"How is the sanctuary?" Dad asked.

"The corridors are flooded, so is the social hall. But miraculously the water stopped right at the sanctuary doors."

Mom's face brightened for the first time that afternoon. "At least we can have the service as planned."

"Only if your guests wear rubber boots and don't mind hiking through six inches of water in their best clothes. The driveway is blocked, the lawn looks like a swamp, the power is off, and the chief of police said it will take a week to clean up."

As Nora offered him a cup of tea, Rabbi Stevens turned to me.

"What do you think about all this?"

What bothered me most, I told him, was that Grandpa wouldn't be able to recite the blessings. I didn't care about the food or flowers. But, whenever I imagined reading before the congregation, I pictured Grandpa sitting in the first row between Mom and Grandma, his lips moving with mine as I chanted my *parashah*.

"We have to make a decision," Rabbi Stevens said. "It's getting late and you have a lot of guests to call. Reverend Michals has offered us the church social hall. The American Legion meeting room is also

available."

"What about the food?" Mom asked. "I can't cook for a hundred people. And the flowers, all those lovely arrangements ruined. We need chairs and tables and plates and silverware. It's too late to rent all of that, it's too late for any of this." Dad put his arm around her.

"Maybe if you simplified your plans," Rabbi Stevens suggested. "Your guests will certainly understand. Perhaps just coffee and dessert."

"We hired a band, waitresses, a woman who specializes in decorations," Mom said. "This is my son's Bar Mitzvah, his entry into manhood. I can't celebrate that with just cookies and Danish. This is awful."

When the phone rang again, Mom jumped. "What now?" she cried. It was Grandma. "Grandpa refuses to stay in bed. He says he feels fine and isn't going to let some Cossack doctor tell him he can't attend his grandson's Bar Mitzvah."

And that's when the idea struck me. "If Grandpa needs to stay in bed, let's take my Bar Mitzvah to him."

"Did you hear that?" Mom said, laughing into the phone. "Alex wants to have his Bar Mitzvah at your house."

Rabbi Stevens looked confused. "Is that an impossible idea? Do

19

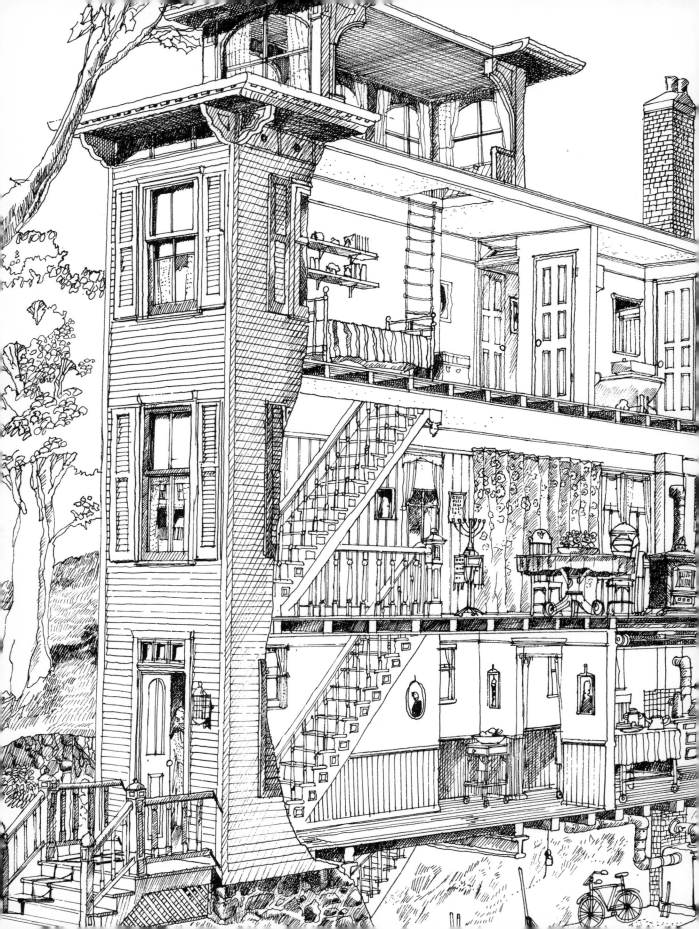

they live in a small apartment?"

"Worse," Mom answered.

Dad laughed. "It's a house, a very special house."

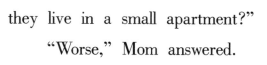

"It's only six feet wide," Mom said. "The oak tree on their front lawn is wider."

Rabbi Stevens thought Mom was joking. "How wide?" he asked. Dad held out his arms curling in the ends of his fingers. The rabbi's eyebrows rose. "Could I see it before we make a decision?"

"Grandpa is supposed to lie quietly in bed for a week," Mom reminded us. "The last thing he needs is a house full of guests. You know how he is when people visit. He'll be giving tours all day, up and down those treacherous stairs."

"Let's show it to the rabbi," Dad said. "Maybe a fresh eye can see new possibilities."

I was rooting for Dad. "You really want your Bar Mitzvah there?" Mom asked. I nodded.

Fifteen minutes later Grandma met us at the narrow door, her face full of worry. "Maybe you can talk some sense into him, Rabbi. He refuses to stay in bed. As soon as he heard you were coming, he started limping around the parlor, trying to rearrange the furniture for tomorrow. If you don't stop him, he'll cripple himself. He won't even take his medicine. Tomorrow he'll wake up so sore he won't be able to walk for weeks."

As she talked she pulled the pins out of her hair and put them in again. "One hundred people here? I don't know how. But, come, Rabbi, take a look. Such matters only a rabbi can decide."

"Why only a rabbi?" Rabbi Stevens asked.

"Because every year you squeeze so many hundreds of people into your tiny sanctuary for the High Holy Days. If you can perform such a miracle there, then maybe you can stretch our house a little too."

We walked into the tiny entrance hall, no bigger than a refrigerator, and then, one at a time, climbed the narrow steps to the second-floor parlor.

Grandpa was trying to move the piano as we entered. When he saw us, he straightened up, adjusted his bathrobe, and limped over with a broad smile on his face.

"You see," he announced, slapping his chest, "perfectly healthy. Welcome, Rabbi. Please excuse my robe."

"Poppa, stop showing off and get into bed," Mom said.

"Too much to do," he remarked, taking Rabbi Stevens by the arm. "Come, let me give you a tour. Alex is a little genius. I've always dreamed of having a Bar Mitzvah or wedding here."

"You see how he limps," Grandma said. "He's in pain. Stop trying to be a hero."

"Sha," Grandpa said. "A little bruise, big deal. Look, Rabbi, from Kolbuszowa, from my grandfather's house." He raised the ancient, dented kiddush cup that always stood between the two candlesticks on the piano. "The first one of my grandchildren to marry gets this cup on their wedding day." Nora blushed. She was the oldest of the cousins. Grandma put her arm around her.

"It certainly is cozy," Rabbi Stevens said, squeezing by the piano to reach the far end of the room.

"When the sun shines, you can't find a more cheerful place in all the world," Grandpa said. Windows lined both walls, filling the room with light. In between the windows, Grandma had hung old, faded photos of her ancestors along with her *ketubah* and a few of the lace collars she had embroidered as a young girl. Rabbi Stevens stopped before each photo.

"But one hundred people!" he murmured to himself. "How could

24

we do it?" He slowly turned around, surveying the room.

"It's crowded just with the seven of us," Mom said.

"Didn't anyone tell you about the annex?" Grandpa asked the rabbi.

"Poppa, don't be silly. We have fifteen minutes to make a decision about your grandson's Bar Mitzvah before I get on the phone and call all our guests. Stop making jokes."

"What jokes, I'm serious. Here we can seat thirty," he waved his arms over the room. "Before the synagogue was built, we once even squeezed almost forty for *Kol Nidre*. The rest we'll seat over here in our special Bar Mitzvah annex."

When he motioned me over to the table, I didn't know whether to take him seriously or not. He had a mischievous gleam in his eyes. "Harold, Rabbi, a hand please." The four of us pushed the heavy table away from the wall. Then Grandpa carefully removed the tapestry hanging there, took a key from his pocket, inserted it into a hole in the wall, told us all to stand back, and slid open the great barn door that had not been used since the piano was delivered through the wall almost fifty years ago.

"Welcome to my annex," he said with a magician's wave of the hand. The seven of us stood in a semicircle near the great sliding door, looking out at the grassy rise on Grandpa's adjacent lot. "Plenty of room out there for all the chairs you want."

"And what if it rains?" Mom asked.

"What rain? It wouldn't dare on my grandson's Bar Mitzvah. Trust me. These aged bones never lie. After living in an ark for fifty years, you get to know when it's going to pour. It may drizzle a little in the morning, but by eleven the sun will shine. Believe me."

Mom did not look convinced. "Does anybody have a better plan?" Dad inquired.

"Where are we going to feed everyone?" Mom asked.

"What's wrong with right there?" Grandpa said, pointing out to the hill. "When Grandma and I were married in Kolbuszowa, we brought all the tables out into the front yard, Uncle Aaron played his clarinet, and everybody sang and danced till dawn, drinking schnapps and eating chicken and kasha."

Mom frowned. "There will be no kasha at my son's Bar Mitzvah."

"Serve what you like. Just stop worrying about rain. I promise you that your guests will never forget Alex's Bar Mitzvah—and neither will you."

For the first time since the flood had forced us to change our plans, there was silence. Mom looked at Dad, Dad looked at the rabbi, and the rabbi peered out through the wall and then studied the long, narrow parlor, trying to imagine it full of people.

"It's up to you, Alex," he said finally. "Should we have your Bar Mitzvah here?"

When I smiled and nodded, Grandpa kissed the top of my head, clapped his hands, and shouted "Done!"

Before sundown, Grandma called all her close friends, asking each to cook something special for the following morning; Dad drove into town to see a client in the office supply business, hoping to get a special delivery of tables and chairs; Rabbi Stevens arranged to have the temple's Torah and prayer books brought to Grandpa's house; and Mom notified all the guests that my Bar Mitzvah would be held not in the temple but at the world's narrowest house. "And bring an umbrella," she said,

28

"just in case."

After the phone calls, Rabbi Stevens and I pushed the sofa platform into the middle of the room and held a brief rehearsal. Then, calling the family together, he told them where to sit and stand during the service, and in what order each would come up for an *aliyah*. When we left, he looked up at the gray sky and said, "I hope your Grandfather is right."

That night I dreamt I was standing on the bow of a tall ship in a great storm. Rain soaked everything, but somehow I remained dry. So did the open Torah which ran around the edge of the deck like a low fence. Far below, Mom, Dad, and Nora sat in a rubber life raft, laughing as if on a roller coaster. I called to them but huge waves kept coming between us, drowning my words. Then suddenly Grandpa limped toward me on a peg leg. He was wearing my clothes, which were too small for him, and trying to find a door in the Torah that led to his parents' house in Kolbuszowa. Twice he walked around the ship, chanting my portion. Then he crouched down, pointed to a Hebrew word in the parchment, winked at me, and disappeared between the letters. Then I awoke.

J ust as Grandpa had predicted, it was overcast and threatening to rain the morning

29

of my Bar Mitzvah. I overheard Mom and Dad talking through the wall. "We were foolish to listen to him," Mom said. "I should have known better." "We had no choice," Dad responded. They both agreed that, if it rained, my Bar Mitzvah would be a disaster. "Oh, Poppa," Mom said, "you'd better be right." A few drops slid down my window.

As I dressed, I imagined the rabbi calling me up to the *bimah*, whispering, "Slowly, don't rush," then stepping to one side. I recited the first blessing, picked up a pencil as if it were the *yad*, placed it on the first word of the dictionary lying open on my desk, and began to recite my Torah portion from memory. After the blessings, I read the *haftarah* and finally ended with my speech, thanking everyone who had helped me to reach that wonderful day, especially my family. Then I shook hands with the desk lamp and collapsed on my bed, imagining the relief I would feel in just a few hours...provided I didn't confuse the blessings.

But I didn't have time to worry about making mistakes. A thousand and one small chores remained before the service began. As I knotted my tie, a huge moving van pulled into the driveway, loaded with tables and chairs. Dad climbed up next to the driver and rode over to Grandpa's to supervise the unloading. There he met Aunt Lilly and Uncle Dave who had gathered enough tablecloths, plates, and silverware from their friends to set all the tables. Meanwhile Mom and Nora ran to the florist for fresh flowers which they arranged in milk bottles covered in tissue paper and ribbons. All morning Grandma's friends arrived with covered pots and casseroles, salad bowls and cookie tins, which she stacked on her narrow kitchen counter. The sweet smell of home-baked pies and roasted meats filled the house.

My assignment was to unload the boxes of prayer books and place one on every chair. By the time I arrived at Grandpa's house, it looked like the ingathering before the flood. Workmen, friends, relatives, and half a dozen dogs were running about, transforming the long-neglected hilltop into a neighborhood festival. The lawn facing the barn door was neatly set with curved rows of armchairs, like an open-air theater. On either side, workmen were rolling out tables and unfolding the legs. Dad stood beside the truck driver who kept scanning the sky and warning, "These chairs aren't meant for outdoors. Rain will ruin them." Dad kept reassuring him, "Don't worry," yet looking up whenever the trees rustled. Over by the tables, Mom muttered, "Poppa!" every time the wind knocked over the flowers.

Inside, Grandma was trying to squeeze one last dish into the refrigerator. "This reminds me of my wedding. The day before Grandpa and I were married, my sisters and I plucked chickens and scraped potatoes till dark. All afternoon, friends dropped in just like this, bringing something special for the party. I enjoyed that afternoon almost as much as my wedding day. Don't tell your mother," she said, dropping her voice to a whisper, "but I'm glad the temple is closed. This is much nicer." Then she kissed me on the forehead and sent me upstairs. Grandpa was looking for me.

He was sitting on the sofa at the far end of the room, his sprained ankle raised, directing the workmen as they carried chairs above their heads. Rabbi Stevens and Cantor Barry stood on the platform before the open barn door, arranging the portable ark and reading table. The ancient kiddush cup and candlesticks from Kolbuszowa had been moved to a small stand beside the ark.

"The guest of honor," Grandpa called as I reached the top of the stairs. "How do you like your *shul*?"

The parlor had been transformed into a sanctuary. "It's amazing," I said, looking around the room. And then suddenly a wonderful feeling washed over me. A miracle was taking place before my eyes. Grandpa's house had become an ark, carrying me across the sea from childhood to the beginning of adulthood. At that moment I lost my nervousness and felt instead a great surge of gratitude for all that everyone was doing to help out.

When I reached him at the far end of the room, Grandpa moved his leg so I could sit beside him. "Nu?" he asked. "How does it feel to become a man?"

"I'm glad the temple flooded," I whispered.

He winked, "Don't tell your mother."

While we sat together, looking down the long room, the sun briefly broke through the clouds and streamed in through the windows. Mom gave a small shout of delight, and Grandpa slapped his knee and laughed, "What did I tell you!"

As the time for the service approached, the parlor became so crowded with family and friends that no one could move. The only way in or out was by the narrow stairs which were blocked by Uncle Arthur whose watch chain had gotten tangled on the banister. New arrivals were waiting downstairs to come up while those upstairs were trying to get down. Dad had run some rope across the opening of the barn door to

keep people from accidently falling out, but my cousin Ralph lost his footing and almost fell. Then Mom cried out, "This is dangerous. Somebody's going to break his neck."

Grandpa rose. "I meant to do this sooner," he said, limping slowly to the barn door and lifting a small hatch in the floor. "Alex, can you kneel down and pull that lever?" he asked, pointing into the darkness. As I did so, I felt the whole house tremble.

"I never did explain why I always called this place my ark," he grinned, as a broad walkway slid slowly out from beneath the floor and onto the grassy hill, touching the ground in front of the seats. It looked like a ship's gangway. All the picture books I'd read of Noah's ark showed the animals coming aboard, two by two, on just such a ramp. "Don't be frightened," he turned to the guests. "It's perfectly safe. That's how we got the piano up here."

Mom was speechless. She had lived in that house for twenty years without knowing about it. "I was saving it for a special occasion," Grandpa said. "You never know when you might need to open your house to the world. This place might be narrow, but it has a big heart. Come, everyone, I think it's time to begin."

Half the guests spilled down the ramp to the lawn while the rest

took their seats in the parlor. A few minutes later, Rabbi Stevens and Cantor Barry stepped onto the *bimah*, and the service began.

When it came time to read from the Torah, Rabbi Stevens called me up to help undress it. Then I stood beside him as, one by one, Grandpa, Grandma, Mom, Dad, and Nora each came up for an *aliyah*. Finally he placed the prayer book before me and whispered, "Slowly." I looked at my family on one side, at my relatives on the other, and out through the barn door at all our friends sitting on the lawn. I didn't want that moment to end. I wanted to hold them all there forever. At that instant, I understood how difficult it must have been for Noah, when the waters receded, to open the doors of the ark. He probably stood on deck a few minutes, hesitating, both grateful for dry land and a little sad at having to say goodbye to everyone.

I lingered a minute, looking at each familiar face. Then it was time to begin. I read the first blessing slowly and carefully, then picked up the *yad*, and began my Torah portion. It all poured out without effort, as if I were singing a familiar song. I recited the *haftarah*, delivered my speech, and then, before I knew it, the song was over and I was dressing the Torah, wondering if I had read too fast, wishing I could begin again.

When the service ended, everyone surrounded me with congratulations, and then we all streamed down the ramp to the garden, clearing the ark of everyone but Grandpa who limped slowly after us. Dad shook my hand and then lifted me off my feet in a great bear hug. Nora said I read better than she had. And Mom kissed both my cheeks and whispered loud enough for Grandpa to hear, "I'm glad we had the service here."

The sun shone brightly all afternoon, just as Grandpa had promised. After lunch, while the adults drank coffee and exchanged news of distant relatives and old friends, Nora and I took our cousins through the house, showing them all its secrets. We ended up in the crow's nest, watching the yellow blinking lights of the repair trucks as they drove about in front of the temple.

When the guests began to leave, I whispered to Grandpa, "I don't want my Bar Mitzvah to end."

"It never will," he smiled. "You'll remember it for the rest of your life. And some day, when your children are preparing to read from the Torah, you'll tell them how years ago an ark saved your Bar Mitzvah from the flood."

GLOSSARY

ALIYAH—the honor of being called up to the *bimah* (see below) to recite the blessings before and after the reading of the Torah.

BAR MITZVAH—both the Jewish boy who on his thirteenth birthday becomes a "son of the commandment" and the ceremony that marks his entry into the adult Jewish community. *(Bat Mitzvah means "daughter of the commandment.")*

BARECHU—"Let us pray," the first word of the prayer recited before the reading of the Torah.

BARUCH—"Blessed," the first word of the prayer recited before the reading of the *haftarah* (see below).

BIMAH—the platform in a synagogue from which the Torah is read.

CHEDER—popular term for an elementary religious school, especially in Eastern Europe.

CHUMASH—the first five books of the Bible, often in a single volume.

HAFTARAH—the selections from the Prophets that are read after the Torah reading on the Sabbath and festivals.

ketubah

KASHA—groats, crushed oats, or wheat.

KETUBAH—a Jewish marriage contract, often beautifully decorated.

kasha

KIDDUSH CUP—usually a finely crafted goblet that holds the wine used in blessing the Sabbath and holy days.

KLEZMER—the Yiddish word for a folk musician.

KOL NIDRE—the opening prayer recited on the eve of Yom Kippur, the Day of Atonement, and generally used to refer to the service itself.

kiddush cup

PARASHAH—the selection from the Torah read every Sabbath.

SCHNAPPS—whiskey.

SHTETL—the Yiddish word for a small Jewish village or town, formerly found in Eastern Europe.

shtetl

SHUL—Yiddish term for synagogue.

SIDRAH—same as *Parashah*.

TORAH—the first five books of the Bible (see *Chumash*), often on a parchment scroll.

YAD—pointer used for indicating one's place when reading from the Torah.